The
Super-str
Tria

by Steve Cole
Illustrated by Bill Ledger

In this story ...

Pip
(Boost)

Pip is super strong! She can lift up really heavy weights, like boulders. She once lifted a skyscraper!

Ben
(Sprint)

Mr Trainer
(teacher)

Chapter 1:
Bring on the Games!

"This is my idea of a morning workout!" said Pip. She was lifting the breakfast table with one hand and adding milk to her cereal with the other.

"You should be saving your strength for later," Ben said.

Pip put the table down. "You're right," she said. "I don't want to let the team down after your amazing victory yesterday."

The day before, Hero Academy had beaten their rivals, Superpower School, in the Superpower Games. Today was the second and final day of the Games, and Pip was competing in the super-strength trials. She changed into her superhero costume and became Boost.

THE SUPERPOWER GAMES

The Superpower Games is the most exciting and important superhero sports competition in the world! Young superheroes compete against each other in a series of thrilling contests, held over two days. The winner of each contest receives a medal.

At the end of the two days, the school with the most medals receives the Superpower Games Cup.

Events include:
- speed test race
- dodgeball
- hover-kart racing
- super-strength trials

As she left the dinner hall and jogged over to the sports ground, Boost thought about the trials ahead. She knew it was going to be a tough competition, but she felt quietly confident … until she saw her opponent.

He was juggling bowling balls as if they weighed nothing.

"My name's Rocko," he said, crushing one of the bowling balls in his hands. "It's a pity our team captain was sent home yesterday," Rocko said. "Blur would have loved to watch me beat you."

"Blur shouldn't have cheated then, should he?" Boost said crossly.

Blur had spied on Hero Academy's training sessions to find out their strengths and weaknesses, but he had been found out.

"Anyway, who says you're going to beat me?" Boost continued.

"I do! You don't stand a chance," Rocko replied with a grin, before heading towards the rest of his team.

"We'll see," Boost called after him.

Boost looked nervously at the crowd of people who had gathered to watch the super-strength trials.

Sprint, who was Hero Academy's team captain, ran up to her. "How are you feeling, Boost?"

Boost sighed and told him about Rocko's boasts.

"Rocko's just trying to make you doubt yourself," said Sprint. "Ignore him."

Just then, a bell rang to signal the start of the trials. The crowd fell silent as the judges – Miss Gatsby and Mr Trainer – walked out. Miss Gatsby was the Power Exploration (PE) teacher at Superpower School and Mr Trainer was Hero Academy's PE teacher.

"Let the super-strength trials begin!" Miss Gatsby cried.

"Good luck, everyone," Mr Trainer added.

Chapter 2: Trial after trial

The first trial of strength was to heave a massive lorry, loaded with heavy weights, up a steep ramp.

Boost's muscles strained as she hauled her lorry up. Rocko staggered beside her, sweating and panting. They were neck-and-neck all the way to the top.

"It's a draw!" cried Miss Gatsby.

The second trial of strength was to bend a long, solid steel bar into a bow.

Boost quickly tied hers up in a neat bow. Rocko did the same, and in the same time.

"Another draw!" said Mr Trainer.

"Well done, Rocko," said Boost.

Rocko scowled. "I'm just warming up."

In the third trial of strength, Boost had to hurl an old piano as far as she could. It landed with a crash on the far side of the arena. Rocko did the same. His piano fell right on top of Boost's. They had tied once more.

"Joint winners," declared Miss Gatsby. "Again!"

"This is ridiculous," muttered Rocko.

Boost and Rocko tied in three more strength trials: 'Juggle the Boulders', 'Knock Down the Fortress' and 'Shatter the Shot Put'.

"There's only one event left," Sprint told Boost. "It's 'Lift the Cars'. You can beat Rocko this time, I know you can."

Boost nodded wearily. Secretly, she wasn't so sure. Her whole body ached.

In the final trial, Boost and Rocko had to hold as many cars over their heads as they could. A huge crane added a new car to the pile every thirty seconds.

Boost lifted the first car and gritted her teeth as the crane dropped more and more vehicles on top of it.

Rocko matched Boost, of course. Eight cars … nine cars …

They kept going until they were up to twenty cars each!

Boost was so tired! She could feel her knees starting to buckle.

Finally – with a *CRASH!* – Rocko dropped all his cars.

"Boost is the winner," Mr Trainer declared. "Hero Academy triumphs again!"

Sprint led the cheering as the crowd went wild.

Boost breathed a big sigh of relief as she put down the cars.

"Bah," said Rocko miserably. "Now I'm glad Blur wasn't here to see me lose."

"It was a great contest," Boost replied. "My legs are trembling now."

"So are mine." Rocko frowned. "Wait. So are my feet. What's going on?"

Mr Trainer ran up to Boost looking very worried. "We have a problem!" he said. "I just went to get your medal, but it's gone. All the medals are gone. The Superpower Games Cup is missing too!"

Boost couldn't believe it. "You mean, someone has stolen them?"

Mr Trainer nodded. "Yes ... There's a thief about!"

Chapter 3:
The mole-machine

"Did anyone see the thief?" Rocko asked Mr Trainer.

"No," Mr Trainer replied, "but there's a huge hole in the floor of the staffroom, where we were keeping the medals."

"Wait," said Boost. "Rocko, you thought your feet were trembling … "

"Now it feels like the *ground* is shaking!" Rocko added.

"You're right," Mr Trainer said. He frowned as the ground shook harder. "Something must be moving beneath us, making the earth shake."

Boost gasped. "Mr Trainer, I think the thief might be using a machine to tunnel underground!"

Just then, the rumble of an engine could be heard beneath them.

VROOM! An enormous machine burst out from the ground beside them. It looked like an armoured car crossed with a mole.

Boost was right in its path! Rocko yanked her out of the way, pulling her to safety just in time.

"Thanks, Rocko," said Boost shakily.

"That's my mole-machine!" cried Miss Gatsby.

"Your what?" asked Boost.

"My mole-machine," Miss Gatsby said. "I invented it so that heroes could break into baddies' underground lairs."

The machine zigzagged over the playing field. It looked as if it was out of control.

"Whoever's inside isn't driving it very well," Boost noted.

The mole-machine smashed into the crane and knocked it down.

"Come on, Rocko," Boost shouted. "We've got to stop that thing!"

Rocko grinned. "Looks like the super-strength trials aren't over yet!"

Boost and Rocko ran after the runaway mole-machine. Boost grabbed hold of the back of it, but it dragged her off balance and she fell flat on her face!

"I'll handle this," said Rocko. He grabbed some of the cars he'd dropped in the last trial and threw them in front of the mole-machine to make a barrier. It made no difference – the mole-machine ploughed right through them.

"Rocko, I have an idea," said Boost, "but we will have to work together."

"Together?" Rocko looked at Boost. "Even though we're on different sides?"

"Right now we both want the same thing," Boost pointed out. "To safely stop that mole-machine before someone gets hurt."

Rocko nodded. "What's your idea?"

Boost pointed to the knocked-over crane. It had an enormous metal hook. "Are you any good at fishing?"

Rocko grinned.

Together, Rocko and Boost pulled the arm off the broken crane. Then, straining and panting, they lifted it up and used it like a massive fishing rod!

The crane's hook clanged against the mole-machine's roof and bounced right off.

"The thief is starting to burrow underground again!" Mr Trainer cried. "Quick, hook the mole-machine, before it's too late!"

Their muscles bulging with effort, Boost and Rocko tried again. This time, the hook snagged on one of the mole-machine's digging claws.

"Now, lift!" Boost bellowed.

Boost and Rocko tilted the arm of the crane and lifted the mole-machine up into the air.

"What a catch!" Rocko grinned as the mole-machine dangled helplessly from the crane.

Miss Gatsby came running over. "I'd like to know who's inside it," she said.

The mole-machine's hatch flipped open … and Blur leaned out from inside. "Put me down," he cried. "I'm scared of heights!"

“Blur!” Miss Gatsby looked shocked. “How could you do this?”

Blur looked ashamed. “After I was disqualified yesterday, I wanted to spoil the Superpower Games,” he admitted.

Boost and Rocko gently lowered the mole-machine and Blur climbed out. A medal fell out of his pocket. “I didn’t mean to cause all this damage,” he said. “I’m sorry.”

Miss Gatsby gave Blur a stern look. “We will have a serious talk later,” she said.

"In the meantime," said Mr Trainer, "we still need to award Boost her medal!"

Mr Trainer got the crowd's attention and announced that Boost was the winner of the super-strength trials. She had never felt happier as the crowd cheered for her.

Mr Trainer called for silence. "We are pleased to announce that the overall winner of the Superpower Games Cup is ..."

"... Hero Academy!" cried Miss Gatsby, handing the cup to Sprint.

Sprint passed it straight to Boost. "I think you should hold this," he said. "Without you, we wouldn't even have a Superpower Games Cup."

Boost blushed, then held the cup up in the air. The crowd cheered and waved.

Later, Boost caught up with Rocko before he got back on his school bus. She tore her super-strength trial medal in two and passed one half to Rocko.

He stared. "Why did you do that?"

"Because we saved the Superpower Games by working together," she said. "You earned this as much as me!"

"Thank you." Rocko said. Then he grinned. "See you next year for a rematch?"

"You bet," replied Boost.